COURAGE

J. M. Barrie

COURAGE

BY

J. M. Barrie

You have had many rectors here in St. Andrews who will continue in bloom long after the lowly ones such as I am are dead and rotten and forgotten. They are the roses in December; you remember someone said that God gave us memory so that we might have roses in December. But I do not envy the great ones. In my experience--and you may find in the end it is yours also--the people I have cared for most and who have seemed most worth caring for--my December roses--have been very simple folk. Yet I wish that for this hour I could swell into someone of importance, so as to do you credit. I suppose you had a melting for me because I was hewn out of one of your own quarries, walked similar academic groves, and have trudged the road on which you will soon set forth. I would that I could put into your hands a staff for that somewhat bloody march, for though there is much about myself that I conceal from other people, to help you I would expose every cranny of my mind.

But, alas, when the hour strikes for the Rector to answer to his call he is unable to become the undergraduate he used to be, and so the only door into you is closed. We, your elders, are much more interested in you than you are in us. We are not really important to you. I have utterly forgotten the address of the Rector of my time, and even who he was, but I recall vividly climbing up a statue to tie his colours round its neck and being hurled therefrom with contumely. We remember the important things. I cannot provide you with that staff for your journey; but perhaps I can tell you a little about it, how to use it and lose it and find it again, and cling to it more than ever. You shall cut it--so it is ordained--every one of you for himself, and its name is Courage. You must excuse me if I talk a good deal about courage to you to-day. There is nothing else much worth speaking about to undergraduates or graduates or white-haired men and women. It is the lovely virtue--the rib of Himself that God sent down to

His children.

My special difficulty is that though you have had literary rectors here before, they were the big guns, the historians, the philosophers; you have had none, I think, who followed my more humble branch, which may be described as playing hide and seek with angels. My puppets seem more real to me than myself, and I could get on much more swingingly if I made one of them deliver this address. It is M'Connachie who has brought me to this pass. M'Connachie, I should explain, as I have undertaken to open the innermost doors, is the name I give to the unruly half of myself: the writing half. We are complement and supplement. I am the half that is dour and practical and canny, he is the fanciful half; my desire is to be the family solicitor, standing firm on my hearthrug among the harsh realities of the office furniture; while he prefers to fly around on one wing. I should not mind him doing that, but he drags me with him. I have sworn that M'Connachie shall not interfere with this address to-day; but there is no telling. I might have done things worth while if it had not been for M'Connachie, and my first piece of advice to you at any rate shall be sound: don't copy me. A good subject for a rectorial address would be the mess the Rector himself has made of life. I merely cast this forth as a suggestion, and leave the working of it out to my successor. I do not think it has been used yet.

My own theme is Courage, as you should use it in the great fight that seems to me to be coming between youth and their betters; by youth, meaning, of course, you, and by your betters us. I want you to take up this position: That youth have for too long left exclusively in our hands the decisions in national matters that are more vital to them than to us. Things about the next war, for instance, and why the last one ever had a beginning. I use the word fight because it must, I think, begin with a challenge; but the aim is the reverse of antagonism, it is partnership. I want you to hold that the time has arrived for youth to demand that partnership, and to demand it courageously. That to gain courage is what you came to St. Andrews for. With some alarums and excursions into college life. That is what I propose, but, of course, the issue lies with M'Connachie.

Your betters had no share in the immediate cause of

the war; we know what nation has that blot to wipe out; but for fifty years or so we heeded not the rumblings of the distant drum, I do not mean by lack of military preparations; and when war did come we told youth, who had to get us out of it, tall tales of what it really is and of the clover beds to which it leads.

We were not meaning to deceive, most of us were as honourable and as ignorant as the youth themselves; but that does not acquit us of failings such as stupidity and jealousy, the two black spots in human nature which, more than love of money, are at the root of all evil. If you prefer to leave things as they are we shall probably fail you again. Do not be too sure that we have learned our lesson, and are not at this very moment doddering down some brimstone path.

I am far from implying that even worse things than war may not come to a State. There are circumstances in which nothing can so well become a land, as I think this land proved when the late war did break out and there was but one thing to do. There is a form of anae-mia that is more rotting than even an unjust war. The end will indeed have come to our courage and to us when we are afraid in dire mischance to refer the final appeal to the arbitrament of arms. I suppose all the lusty of our race, alive and dead, join hands on that.

'And he is dead who will not fight;
And who dies fighting has increase.'

But if you must be in the struggle, the more reason you should know why, before it begins, and have a say in the decision whether it is to begin. The youth who went to the war had no such knowledge, no such say; I am sure the survivors, of whom there must be a number here to-day, want you to be wiser than they were, and are certainly determined to be wiser next time themselves. If you are to get that partnership, which, once gained, is to be for mutual benefit, it will be, I should say, by banding yourselves with these men, not defiantly but firmly, not for selfish ends but for your country's good. In the meantime they have one bulwark; they have a General who is befriending them as I think never, after the fighting was over, has a General befriended his men before. Perhaps the seemly thing would be for us, their betters, to elect one of these young survivors of the carnage to be our Rector. He ought now to know a few things about war that are worth our hearing. If his theme were the Rector's favourite, diligence. I should be afraid of his advising a great many of us to be diligent in sitting still and doing no more harm.

Of course he would put it more suavely than that, though it is not, I think, by gentleness that you will get your rights; we are dogged ones at sticking to what we have got, and so will you be at our age. But avoid calling us ugly names; we may be stubborn and we may be blunderers, but we love you more than aught else in the world, and once you have won your partnership we shall all be welcoming you. I urge you not to use ugly names about anyone. In the war it was not the fighting men who were distinguished for abuse; as has been well said, 'Hell hath no fury like a non-combatant.' Never ascribe to an opponent motives meaner than your own. There may be students here to-day who have decided this session to go in for immortality, and would like to know of an easy way of accomplishing it. That is a way, but not so easy as you think. Go through life without ever ascribing to your opponents motives meaner than your own. Nothing so lowers the moral currency; give it up, and be great.

Another sure way to fame is to know what you mean. It is a solemn thought that almost no one--if he is truly eminent--knows what he means. Look at the great ones of the earth, the politicians. We do not discuss what they say, but what they may have meant when they said it. In 1922 we are all wondering, and so are they, what they meant in 1914 and afterwards. They are publishing books trying to find out; the men of action as well as the men of words. There are exceptions. It is not that our statesmen are 'sugared mouths with minds therefrae'; many of them are the best men we have got, upright and anxious, nothing cheaper than to miscall them. The explanation seems just to be that it is so difficult to know what you mean, especially when you have become a swell. No longer apparently can you deal in 'russet yeas and honest kersey noes'; gone for ever is simplicity, which is as beautiful as the divine plain face of Lamb's Miss Kelly. Doubts breed suspicions, a dangerous air. Without suspicion there might have been no war. When you are called to Downing Street to discuss what you want of your betters with the Prime Minister he won't be suspicious, not as far as you can see; but remember the atmosphere of generations you are in, and when he passes you the toast-rack say to yourselves, if you would be in the mode, 'Now, I wonder what he means by that.'

Even without striking out in the way I suggest, you are already disturbing your betters considerably. I sometimes talk this over with M'Connachie, with whom, as you may guess, circumstances compel me to pass a good deal of my time. In our talks we agree that we, your betters, constantly find you forgetting that we are your betters. Your answer is that the war and other happenings have shown you that age is not necessarily another name for sapience; that our avoidance of frankness in life and in the arts is often, but not so often as you think, a cowardly way of shirking unpalatable truths, and that you have taken us off our pedestals because we look more natural on the ground. You who are at the rash age even accuse your elders, sometimes not without justification, of being more rash than yourselves. 'If Youth but only knew,' we used to teach you to sing; but now, just because Youth has been to the war, it wants to change the next line into 'If Age had only to do.'

In so far as this attitude of yours is merely passive, sullen, negative, as it mainly is, despairing of our capacity and anticipating a future of gloom, it is no game for man or woman. It is certainly the opposite of that for which I plead. Do not stand aloof, despising, disbelieving, but come in and help--insist on coming in and helping. After all, we have shown a good deal of courage; and your part is to add a greater courage to it. There are glorious years lying ahead of you if you choose to make them glorious. God's in His Heaven still. So forward, brave hearts. To what adventures I cannot tell, but I know that your God is watching to see whether you are adventurous. I know that the great partnership is only a first step, but I do not know what are to be the next and the next. The partnership is but a tool; what are you to do with it? Very little, I warn you, if you are merely thinking of yourselves; much if what is at the marrow of your thoughts is a future that even you can scarcely hope to see.

Learn as a beginning how world-shaking situations arise and how they may be countered. Doubt all your betters who would deny you that right of partnership. Begin by doubting all such in high places-- except, of course, your professors. But doubt all other professors-- yet not conceitedly, as some do, with their noses in the air; avoid all such physical risks. If it necessitates your pushing some of us out of our places, still push; you will find it needs some shoving. But the things courage can do! The things that even incompetence can do if it works with singleness of purpose. The war has done at least one big thing: it has taken spring out of the year. And, this accomplished, our leading people are amazed to find that the other seasons are not conducting themselves as usual. The spring of the year lies buried in the fields of France and elsewhere. By the time the next eruption comes it may be you who are responsible for it and your sons who are in the lava. All, perhaps, because this year you let things slide.

We are a nice and kindly people, but it is already evident that we are stealing back into the old grooves, seeking cushions for our old bones, rather than attempting to build up a fairer future. That is what we mean when we say that the country is settling down. Make haste, or you will become like us, with only the thing we proudly call experience to add to your stock, a poor exchange for the generous feelings that time will take away. We have no intention of giving you your share. Look around and see how much share Youth has now that the war is over. You got a handsome share while it lasted.

I expect we shall beat you; unless your fortitude be doubly girded by a desire to send a message of cheer to your brothers who fell, the only message, I believe, for which they crave; they are not worrying about their Aunt Jane. They want to know if you have learned wisely from what befell them; if you have, they will be braced in the feeling that they did not die in vain. Some of them think they did. They will not take our word for it that they did not. You are their living image; they know you could not lie to them, but they distrust our flattery and our cunning faces. To us they have passed away; but are you who stepped into their heritage only yesterday, whose books are scarcely cold to their hands, you who still hear their cries being blown across the links--are you already relegating them to the shades?

The gaps they have left in this University are among the most honourable of her wounds. But we are not here to acclaim them. Where they are now, hero is, I think, a very little word. They call to you to find out in time the truth about this great game, which your elders play for stakes and Youth plays for its life.

I do not know whether you are grown a little tired of that word hero, but I am sure the heroes are. That is the subject of one of our unfinished plays; M'Connachie is the one who writes the plays. If any one of you here proposes to be a playwright you can take this for your own and finish it. The scene is a school, schoolmasters present, but if you like you could make it a university, professors present. They are discussing an illuminated scroll about a student fallen in the war, which they have kindly presented to his parents; and unexpectedly the parents enter. They are an old pair, backbent, they have been stalwarts in their day but have now gone small; they are poor, but not so poor that they could not send their boy to college. They are in black, not such a rusty black either, and you may be sure she is the one who knows what to do with his hat. Their faces are gnarled, I suppose--but I do not need to describe that pair to Scottish students. They have come to thank the Senatus for their lovely scroll and to ask them to tear it up. At first they had been enamoured to read of what a scholar their son was, how noble and adored by all. But soon a fog settled over them, for this grand person was not the boy they knew. He had many a fault well known to them; he was not always so noble; as a scholar he did no more than scrape through; and he sometimes made his father rage and his mother grieve. They had liked to talk such memories as these together, and smile over them, as if they were bits of him he had left lying about the house. So thank you kindly, and would you please give them back their boy by tearing up the scroll? I see nothing else for our dramatist to do. I think he should ask an alumna of St. Andrews to play the old lady (indicating Miss Ellen Terry). The loveliest of all young actresses, the dearest of all old ones; it seems only yesterday that all the men of imagination proposed to their beloveds in some such frenzied words as these, 'As I can't get Miss Terry, may I have you?'

This play might become historical as the opening of

your propaganda in the proposed campaign. How to
make a practical advance? The League of Nations is a
very fine thing, but it cannot save you, because it will
be run by us. Beware your betters bringing presents.
What is wanted is something run by yourselves. You
have more in common with the Youth of other lands
than Youth and Age can ever have with each other;
even the hostile countries sent out many a son very like
ours, from the same sort of homes, the same sort of universities, who had as little to do as our youth had with
the origin of the great adventure. Can we doubt that
many of these on both sides who have gone over and
were once opponents are now friends? You ought to
have a League of Youth of all countries as your beginning, ready to say to all Governments, 'We will fight
each other but only when we are sure of the necessity.'
Are you equal to your job, you young men? If not, I call
upon the red-gowned women to lead the way. I sound
to myself as if I were advocating a rebellion, though I
am really asking for a larger friendship. Perhaps I may
be arrested on leaving the hall. In such a cause I should
think that I had at last proved myself worthy to be your

Rector.

You will have to work harder than ever, but possibly not so much at the same things; more at modern languages certainly if you are to discuss that League of Youth with the students of other nations when they come over to St. Andrews for the Conference. I am far from taking a side against the classics. I should as soon argue against your having tops to your heads; that way lie the best tops. Science, too, has at last come to its own in St. Andrews. It is the surest means of teaching you how to know what you mean when you say. So you will have to work harder. Isaak Walton quotes the saying that doubtless the Almighty could have created a finer fruit than the strawberry, but that doubtless also He never did. Doubtless also He could have provided us with better fun than hard work, but I don't know what it is. To be born poor is probably the next best thing. The greatest glory that has ever come to me was to be swallowed up in London, not knowing a soul, with no means of subsistence, and the fun of working till the stars went out. To have known any one would have spoilt it. I did not even quite know the language. I rang for my boots, and they thought I said a glass of water, so I drank the water and worked on. There was no food in the cupboard, so I did not need to waste time in eating. The pangs and agonies when no proof came. How courteously tolerant was I of the postman without a proof for us; how M'Connachie, on the other hand, wanted to punch his head. The magic days when our article appeared in an evening paper. The promptitude with which I counted the lines to see how much we should get for it. Then M'Connachie's superb air of dropping it into the gutter. Oh, to be a free lance of journalism again--that darling jade! Those were days. Too good to last. Let us be grave. Here comes a Rector.

But now, on reflection, a dreadful sinking assails me, that this was not really work. The artistic callings--you remember how Stevenson thumped them--are merely doing what you are clamorous to be at; it is not real work unless you would rather be doing something else. My so-called labours were just M'Connachie running away with me again. Still, I have sometimes worked; for instance, I feel that I am working at this moment. And the big guns are in the same plight as the little ones.

Carlyle, the king of all rectors, has always been accepted as the arch-apostle of toil, and has registered his many woes. But it will not do. Despite sickness, poortith, want and all, he was grinding all his life at the one job he revelled in. An extraordinarily happy man, though there is no direct proof that he thought so.

There must be many men in other callings besides the arts lauded as hard workers who are merely out for enjoyment. Our Chancellor? (indicating Lord Haig). If our Chancellor has always a passion to be a soldier, we must reconsider him as a worker. Even our Principal? How about the light that burns in our Principal's room after decent people have gone to bed? If we could climb up and look in--I should like to do something of that kind for the last time--should we find him engaged in honest toil, or guiltily engrossed in chemistry?

You will all fall into one of those two callings, the joyous or the uncongenial; and one wishes you into the first, though our sympathy, our esteem, must go rather to the less fortunate, the braver ones who 'turn their necessity to glorious gain' after they have put away their dreams. To the others will go the easy prizes of life,

success, which has become a somewhat odious onion
nowadays, chiefly because we so often give the name
to the wrong thing. When you reach the evening of
your days you will, I think, see--with, I hope, becoming cheerfulness--that we are all failures, at least all the
best of us. The greatest Scotsman that ever lived wrote
himself down a failure:

'The poor inhabitant below
Was quick to learn and wise to know
And keenly felt the friendly glow
And softer flame.
But thoughtless follies laid him low,
And stained his name.'

Perhaps the saddest lines in poetry, written by a man
who could make things new for the gods themselves.

If you want to avoid being like Burns there are several possible ways. Thus you might copy us, as we shine
forth in our published memoirs, practically without a
flaw. No one so obscure nowadays but that he can have
a book about him. Happy the land that can produce
such subjects for the pen.

But do not put your photograph at all ages into your

autobiography. That may bring you to the ground. 'My Life; and what I have done with it'; that is the sort of title, but it is the photographs that give away what you have done with it. Grim things, those portraits; if you could read the language of them you would often find it unnecessary to read the book. The face itself, of course, is still more tell-tale, for it is the record of all one's past life. There the man stands in the dock, page by page; we ought to be able to see each chapter of him melting into the next like the figures in the cinematograph. Even the youngest of you has got through some chapters already. When you go home for the next vacation someone is sure to say 'John has changed a little; I don't quite see in what way, but he has changed.' You remember they said that last vacation. Perhaps it means that you look less like your father. Think that out. I could say some nice things of your betters if I chose.

In youth you tend to look rather frequently into a mirror, not at all necessarily from vanity. You say to yourself, 'What an interesting face; I wonder what he is to be up to?' Your elders do not look into the mirror so often. We know what he has been up to. As yet there is unfortunately no science of reading other people's faces; I think a chair for this should be founded in St. Andrews.

The new professor will need to be a sublime philosopher, and for obvious reasons he ought to wear spectacles before his senior class. It will be a gloriously optimistic chair, for he can tell his students the glowing truth, that what their faces are to be like presently depends mainly on themselves. Mainly, not altogether--

'I am the master of my fate,

I am the captain of my soul.'

I found the other day an old letter from Henley that told me of the circumstances in which he wrote that poem. 'I was a patient,' he writes, 'in the old infirmary of Edinburgh. I had heard vaguely of Lister, and went there as a sort of forlorn hope on the chance of saving my foot. The great surgeon received me, as he did and does everybody, with the greatest kindness, and for twenty months I lay in one or other ward of the old place under his care. It was a desperate business, but he saved my foot, and here I am.' There he was, ladies and gentlemen, and what he was doing during that 'desperate business' was singing that he was master of his fate.

   If you want an example of courage try Henley. Or Stevenson. I could tell you some stories abut these two, but they would not be dull enough for a rectorial address. For courage, again, take Meredith, whose laugh was 'as broad as a thousand beeves at pasture.' Take, as I think, the greatest figure literature has still left us, to be added to-day to the roll of St. Andrews' alumni, though it must be in absence. The pomp and circumstance of war will pass, and all others now alive may fade from the scene, but I think the quiet figure of Hardy will live on.

   I seem to be taking all my examples from the calling I was lately pretending to despise. I should like to read you some passages of a letter from a man of another calling, which I think will hearten you. I have the little filmy sheets here. I thought you might like to see the actual letter; it has been a long journey; it has been to the South Pole. It is a letter to me from Captain Scott of the Antarctic, and was written in the tent you know of, where it was found long afterwards with his body and those of some other very gallant gentlemen, his com-

rades. The writing is in pencil, still quite clear, though
toward the end some of the words trail away as into the
great silence that was waiting for them. It begins:

'We are pegging out in a very comfortless spot.

Hoping this letter may be found and sent to you, I
write

you a word of farewell. I want you to think well of
me

and my end.' (After aome private instructions too
intimate to read, he goes on): 'Goodbye--I am not at
all afraid of the end, but sad to miss many a simple
pleasure which I had planned for the future in our
long marches. . . .

We are in a desperate state--feet
frozen, etc., no fuel, and a long way from food, but
it

would do your heart good to be in our tent, to hear
our

songs and our cheery conversation. . . . Later--(it
is here that the words become difficult)--We are
very

near the end. . . . We did intend to finish ourselves

when things proved like this, but we have decided to die

naturally without.'

I think it may uplift you all to stand for a moment by that tent and listen, as he says, to their songs and cheery conversation. When I think of Scott I remember the strange Alpine story of the youth who fell down a glacier and was lost, and of how a scientific companion, one of several who accompanied him, all young, computed that the body would again appear at a certain date and place many years afterwards. When that time came round some of the survivors returned to the glacier to see if the prediction would be fulfilled; all old men now; and the body reappeared as young as on the day he left them. So Scott and his comrades emerge out of the white immensities always young.

How comely a thing is affliction borne cheerfully, which is not beyond the reach of the humblest of us. What is beauty? It is these hard-bitten men singing courage to you from their tent; it is the waves of their island home crooning of their deeds to you who are to follow them. Sometimes beauty boils over and them spirits are abroad. Ages may pass as we look or listen, for time is annihilated. There is a very old legend told to me by Nansen the explorer--I like well to be in the company of explorers--the legend of a monk who had wandered into the fields and a lark began to sing. He had never heard a lark before, and he stood there entranced until the bird and its song had become part of the heavens. Then he went back to the monastery and found there a doorkeeper whom he did not know and who did not know him. Other monks came, and they were all strangers to him. He told them he was Father Anselm, but that was no help. Finally they looked through the books of the monastery, and these revealed that there had been a Father Anselm there a hundred or more years before. Time had been blotted out while he listened to the lark.

That, I suppose, was a case of beauty boiling over, or a soul boiling over; perhaps the same thing. Then spirits walk.

They must sometimes walk St. Andrews. I do not mean the ghosts of queens or prelates, but one that keeps step, as soft as snow, with some poor student. He sometimes catches sight of it. That is why his fellows can never quite touch him, their best beloved; he half knows something of which they know nothing--the secret that is hidden in the face of the Monna Lisa. As I see him, life is so beautiful to him that its proportions are monstrous. Perhaps his childhood may have been overfull of gladness; they don't like that. If the seekers were kind he is the one for whom the flags of his college would fly one day. But the seeker I am thinking of is unfriendly, and so our student is 'the lad that will never be told.' He often gaily forgets, and thinks he has slain his foe by daring him, like him who, dreading water, was always the first to leap into it. One can see him serene, astride a Scotch cliff, singing to the sun the farewell thanks of a boy:

'Throned on a cliff serene Man saw the sun
hold a red torch above the farthest seas,
and the fierce island pinnacles put on
in his defence their sombre panoplies;
Foremost the white mists eddied, trailed and spun
like seekers, emulous to clasp his knees,
till all the beauty of the scene seemed one,

led by the secret whispers of the breeze.
'The sun's torch suddenly flashed upon his face
and died; and he sat content in subject night
and dreamed of an old dead foe that had sought
and found him;
a beast stirred bodly in his resting-place;
And the cold came; Man rose to his master-height,
shivered, and turned away; but the mists were
round him.'

If there is any of you here so rare that the seekers have taken an ill-will to him, as to the boy who wrote those lines, I ask you to be careful. Henley says in that poem we were speaking of:
'Under the bludgeonings of Chance
My head is bloody but unbowed.'

A fine mouthful, but perhaps 'My head is bloody and bowed' is better.

Let us get back to that tent with its songs and cheery conversation. Courage. I do not think it is to be got by your becoming solemn-sides before your time. You must have been warned against letting the golden hours slip by. Yes, but some of them are golden only because we let them slip. Diligence--ambition; noble words, but only if 'touched to fine issues.' Prizes may be dross, learning lumber, unless they bring you into the arena with increased understanding. Hanker not too much after worldly prosperity--that corpulent cigar; if you became a millionaire you would probably go swimming around for more like a diseased goldfish. Look to it that what you are doing is not merely toddling to a competency. Perhaps that must be your fate, but fight it and then, though you fail, you may still be among the elect of whom we have spoken. Many a brave man has had to come to it at last. But there are the complacent toddlers from the start. Favour them not, ladies, especially now that every one of you carries a possible marechal's baton under her gown. 'Happy,' it has been said by a distinguished man, 'is he who can leave college with an unreproaching conscience and an unsullied heart.' I don't know; he sounds to me like a sloppy, watery sort of fellow; happy, perhaps, but if there be red blood in him impossible. Be not disheartened by ideals of perfection which can be achieved only by those who run away. Nature, that 'thrifty goddess,' never gave you 'the smallest scruple of her excellence' for that. Whatev-er bludgeonings may be gathering for you, I think one feels more poignantly at your age than ever again in life. You have not our December roses to help you; but you have June coming, whose roses do not wonder, as do ours even while they give us their fragrance--won-dering most when they give us most--that we should linger on an empty scene. It may indeed be monstrous but possibly courageous.

Courage is the thing. All goes if courage goes. What says our glorious Johnson of courage: 'Unless a man has that virtue he has no security for preserving any oth-er.' We should thank our Creator three times daily for courage instead of for our bread, which, if we work, is surely the one thing we have a right to claim of Him. This courage is a proof of our immortality, greater even than gardens 'when the eve is cool.' Pray for it. 'Who rises from prayer a better man, his prayer is answered.' Be not merely courageous, but light-hearted and gay. There is an officer who was the first of our Army to land at Gallipoli. He was dropped overboard to light decoys on the shore, so as to deceive the Turks as to where the landing was to be. He pushed a raft containing these in front of him. It was a frosty night, and he was naked and painted black. Firing from the ships was going on all around. It was a two-hours' swim in pitch darkness. He did it, crawled through the scrub to listen to the talk of the enemy, who were so near that he could have shaken hands with them, lit his decoys and swam back. He seems to look on this as a gay affair. He is a V.C. now, and you would not think to look at him that he could ever have presented such a disreputable appearance. Would you? (indicating Colonel Freyberg).

Those men of whom I have been speaking as the kind to fill the fife could all be light-hearted on occasion. I remember Scott by Highland streams trying to rouse me by maintaining that haggis is boiled bagpipes; Henley in dispute as to whether, say, Turgenieff or Tolstoi could hang the other on his watch-chain; he sometimes clenched the argument by casting his crutch at you; Stevenson responded in the same gay spirit by giving that crutch to John Silver; you remember with what adequate results. You must cultivate this light-heartedness if you are to hang your betters on your watch-chains.

Dr. Johnson--let us have him again-- does not seem to have discovered in his travels that the Scots are a light-hearted nation. Boswell took him to task for saying that the death of Garrick had eclipsed the gaiety of nations. 'Well, sir,' Johnson said, 'there may be occasions when it is permissible to,' etc. But Boswell would not let go. 'I cannot see, sir, how it could in any case have eclipsed the gaiety of nations, as England was the only nation before whom he had ever played.' Johnson was really stymied, but you would never have known it. 'Well, sir,' he said, holing out, 'I understand that Garrick once played in Scotland, and if Scotland has any gaiety to eclipse, which, sir, I deny----'

Prove Johnson wrong for once at the Students' Union and in your other societies. I much regret that there was no Students' Union at Edinburgh in my time. I hope you are fairly noisy and that members are sometimes let out. Do you keep to the old topics? King Charles's head; and Bacon wrote Shakespeare, or if he did not he missed the opportunity of his life. Don't forget to speak scornfully of the Victorian age; there will be time for meekness when you try to better it. Very soon you will be

Victorian or that sort of thing yourselves; next session probably, when the freshmen come up. Afterwards, if you go in for my sort of calling, don't begin by thinking you are the last word in art; quite possibly you are not; steady yourself by remembering that there were great men before William K. Smith. Make merry while you may. Yet light-heartedness is not for ever and a day. At its best it is the gay companion of innocence; and when innocence goes-- as it must go--they soon trip off together, looking for something younger. But courage comes all the way:

'Fight on, my men, says Sir Andrew Barton,
I am hurt, but I am not slaine;
I'll lie me down and bleed a-while,
And then I'll rise and fight againe.'

Another piece of advice; almost my last. For reasons you may guess I must give this in a low voice. Beware of M'Connachie. When I look in a mirror now it is his face I see. I speak with his voice. I once had a voice of my own, but nowadays I hear it from far away only, a melancholy, lonely, lost little pipe. I wanted to be an explorer, but he willed otherwise. You will all have your M'Connachies luring you off the high road. Unless you are constantly on the watch, you will find that he has slowly pushed you out of yourself and taken your place. He has rather done for me. I think in his youth he must somehow have guessed the future and been fleggit by it, flichtered from the nest like a bird, and so our eggs were left, cold. He has clung to me, less from mischief than for companionship; I half like him and his penny whistle; with all his faults he is as Scotch as peat; he whispered to me just now that you elected him, not me, as your Rector.

A final passing thought. Were an old student given an hour in which to revisit the St. Andrews of his day, would he spend more than half of it at lectures? He is more likely to be heard clattering up bare stairs in search of old companions. But if you could choose your hour from all the five hundred years of this seat of learning, wandering at your will from one age to another, how would you spend it? A fascinating theme; so many notable shades at once astir that St. Leonard's and St. Mary's grow murky with them. Hamilton, Melville, Sharpe, Chalmers, down to Herkless, that distin-

guished Principal, ripe scholar and warm friend, the
loss of whom I deeply deplore with you. I think if that
hour were mine, and though at St. Andrews he was but
a passer-by, I would give a handsome part of it to a walk
with Doctor Johnson. I should like to have the time of
day passed to me in twelve languages by the Admirable
Crichton. A wave of the hand to Andrew Lang; and
then for the archery butts with the gay Montrose, all
a-ruffled and ringed, and in the gallant St. Andrews student manner, continued as I understand to this present
day, scattering largess as he rides along,

'But where is now the courtly troupe
That once went riding by?
 I miss the curls of Canteloupe,
The laugh of Lady Di.'

We have still left time for a visit to a house in South
Street, hard by St. Leonard's. I do not mean the house
you mean. I am a Knox man. But little will that avail,
for M'Connachie is a Queen Mary man. So, after all, it
is at her door we chap, a last futile effort to bring that
woman to heel. One more house of call, a student's
room, also in South Street. I have chosen my student,

you see, and I have chosen well; him that sang--

'Life has not since been wholly vain,
And now I bear
Of wisdom plucked from joy and pain
 Some slender share.
'But howsoever rich the store,
I'd lay it down
To feel upon my back once more
The old red gown.'

Well, we have at last come to an end. Some of you may remember when I began this address; we are all older now. I thank you for your patience. This is my first and last public appearance, and I never could or would have made it except to a gathering of Scottish students. If I have concealed my emotions in addressing you it is only the thrawn national way that deceives everybody except Scotsmen. I have not been as dull as I could have wished to be; but looking at your glowing faces cheerfulness and hope would keep breaking through. Despite the imperfections of your betters we leave you a great inheritance, for which others will one day call you to account. You come of a race of men the very wind of whose name has swept to the ultimate seas. Remember--

'Heaven doth with us as we with torches do,

Not light them for themselves. . . .'

Mighty are the Universities of Scotland, and they will prevail. But even in your highest exultations never forget that they are not four, but five. The greatest of them is the poor, proud homes you come out of, which said so long ago: 'There shall be education in this land.' She, not St. Andrews, is the oldest University in Scotland, and all the others are her whelps.

In bidding you good-bye, my last words must be of the lovely virtue. Courage, my children and 'greet the unseen with a cheer.' 'Fight on, my men,' said Sir Andrew Barton. Fight on--you-- for the old red gown till the whistle blows.

The Codes Of Hammurabi And Moses
W. W. Davies

QTY

The discovery of the Hammurabi Code is one of the greatest achievements of archaeology, and is of paramount interest, not only to the student of the Bible, but also to all those interested in ancient history...

Religion   **ISBN:** *1-59462-338-4*   **Pages:**132
MSRP *$12.95*

The Theory of Moral Sentiments
Adam Smith

QTY

This work from 1749. contains original theories of conscience amd moral judgment and it is the foundation for systemof morals.

Philosophy **ISBN:** *1-59462-777-0*   **Pages:**536
MSRP *$19.95*

Jessica's First Prayer
Hesba Stretton

QTY

In a screened and secluded corner of one of the many railway-bridges which span the streets of London there could be seen a few years ago, from five o'clock every morning until half past eight, a tidily set-out coffee-stall, consisting of a trestle and board, upon which stood two large tin cans, with a small fire of charcoal burning under each so as to keep the coffee boiling during the early hours of the morning when the work-people were thronging into the city on their way to their daily toil...

Childrens **ISBN:** *1-59462-373-2*   **Pages:**84
MSRP *$9.95*

My Life and Work
Henry Ford

QTY

Henry Ford revolutionized the world with his implementation of mass production for the Model T automobile. Gain valuable business insight into his life and work with his own auto-biography... "We have only started on our development of our country we have not as yet, with all our talk of wonderful progress, done more than scratch the surface. The progress has been wonderful enough but..."

Biographies/ **ISBN:** *1-59462-198-5*   **Pages:**300
MSRP *$21.95*

The Art of Cross-Examination
Francis Wellman

QTY

I presume it is the experience of every author, after his first book is published upon an important subject, to be almost overwhelmed with a wealth of ideas and illustrations which could readily have been included in his book, and which to his own mind, at least, seem to make a second edition inevitable. Such certainly was the case with me; and when the first edition had reached its sixth impression in five months, I rejoiced to learn that it seemed to my publishers that the book had met with a sufficiently favorable reception to justify a second and considerably enlarged edition. ..

Reference   **ISBN:** *1-59462-647-2*

Pages:412
MSRP $19.95

On the Duty of Civil Disobedience
Henry David Thoreau

QTY

Thoreau wrote his famous essay, On the Duty of Civil Disobedience, as a protest against an unjust but popular war and the immoral but popular institution of slave-owning. He did more than write—he declined to pay his taxes, and was hauled off to gaol in consequence. Who can say how much this refusal of his hastened the end of the war and of slavery ?

Law   **ISBN:** *1-59462-747-9*

Pages:48
MSRP $7.45

Dream Psychology Psychoanalysis for Beginners
Sigmund Freud

QTY

Sigmund Freud, born Sigismund Schlomo Freud (May 6, 1856 - September 23, 1939), was a Jewish-Austrian neurologist and psychiatrist who co-founded the psychoanalytic school of psychology. Freud is best known for his theories of the unconscious mind, especially involving the mechanism of repression; his redefinition of sexual desire as mobile and directed towards a wide variety of objects; and his therapeutic techniques, especially his understanding of transference in the therapeutic relationship and the presumed value of dreams as sources of insight into unconscious desires.

Psychology   **ISBN:** *1-59462-905-6*

Pages:196
MSRP $15.45

The Miracle of Right Thought
Orison Swett Marden

QTY

Believe with all of your heart that you will do what you were made to do. When the mind has once formed the habit of holding cheerful, happy, prosperous pictures, it will not be easy to form the opposite habit. It does not matter how improbable or how far away this realization may see, or how dark the prospects may be, if we visualize them as best we can, as vividly as possible, hold tenaciously to them and vigorously struggle to attain them, they will gradually become actualized, realized in the life. But a desire, a longing without endeavor, a yearning abandoned or held indifferently will vanish without realization.

Self Help   **ISBN:** *1-59462-644-8*

Pages:360
MSRP $25.45

The Rosicrucian Cosmo-Conception Mystic Christianity *by Max Heindel*   ISBN: *1-59462-188-8*   **$38.95**
The Rosicrucian Cosmo-conception is not dogmatic, neither does it appeal to any other authority than the reason of the student. It is: not controversial, but is: sent forth in the, hope that it may help to clear...   *New Age/Religion Pages 646*

Abandonment To Divine Providence *by Jean-Pierre de Caussade*   ISBN: *1-59462-228-0*   **$25.95**
"The Rev. Jean Pierre de Caussade was one of the most remarkable spiritual writers of the Society of Jesus in France in the 18th Century. His death took place at Toulouse in 1751. His works have gone through many editions and have been republished...   *Inspirational/Religion Pages 400*

Mental Chemistry *by Charles Haanel*   ISBN: *1-59462-192-6*   **$23.95**
Mental Chemistry allows the change of material conditions by combining and appropriately utilizing the power of the mind. Much like applied chemistry creates something new and unique out of careful combinations of chemicals the mastery of mental chemistry...   *New Age Pages 354*

The Letters of Robert Browning and Elizabeth Barret Barrett 1845-1846 vol II   ISBN: *1-59462-193-4*   **$35.95**
by Robert Browning and Elizabeth Barrett   *Biographies Pages 596*

Gleanings In Genesis (volume I) *by Arthur W. Pink*   ISBN: *1-59462-130-4*   **$27.45**
Appropriately has Genesis been termed "the seed plot of the Bible" for in it we have, in germ form, almost all of the great doctrines which are afterwards fully developed in the books of Scripture which follow...   *Religion/Inspirational Pages 420*

The Master Key *by L. W. de Laurence*   ISBN: *1-59462-001-6*   **$30.95**
In no branch of human knowledge has there been a more lively increase of the spirit of research during the past few years than in the study of Psychology, Concentration and Mental Discipline. The requests for authentic lessons in Thought Control, Mental Discipline and...   *New Age/Business Pages 422*

The Lesser Key Of Solomon Goetia *by L. W. de Laurence*   ISBN: *1-59462-092-X*   **$9.95**
This translation of the first book of the "Lernegton" which is now for the first time made accessible to students of Talismanic Magic was done, after careful collation and edition, from numerous Ancient Manuscripts in Hebrew, Latin, and French...   *New Age/Occult Pages 92*

Rubaiyat Of Omar Khayyam *by Edward Fitzgerald*   ISBN:*1-59462-332-5*   **$13.95**
Edward Fitzgerald, whom the world has already learned, in spite of his own efforts to remain within the shadow of anonymity, to look upon as one of the rarest poets of the century, was born at Bredfield, in Suffolk, on the 31st of March, 1809. He was the third son of John Purcell...   *Music Pages 172*

Ancient Law *by Henry Maine*   ISBN: *1-59462-128-4*   **$29.95**
The chief object of the following pages is to indicate some of the earliest ideas of mankind, as they are reflected in Ancient Law, and to point out the relation of those ideas to modern thought.   *Religiom/History Pages 452*

Far-Away Stories *by William J. Locke*   ISBN: *1-59462-129-2*   **$19.45**
"Good wine needs no bush, but a collection of mixed vintages does. And this book is just such a collection. Some of the stories I do not want to remain buried for ever in the museum files of dead magazine-numbers an author's not unpardonable vanity..."   *Fiction Pages 272*

Life of David Crockett *by David Crockett*   ISBN: *1-59462-250-7*   **$27.45**
"Colonel David Crockett was one of the most remarkable men of the times in which he lived. Born in humble life, but gifted with a strong will, an indomitable courage, and unremitting perseverance...   *Biographies/New Age Pages 424*

Lip-Reading *by Edward Nitchie*   ISBN: *1-59462-206-X*   **$25.95**
Edward B. Nitchie, founder of the New York School for the Hard of Hearing, now the Nitchie School of Lip-Reading, Inc, wrote "LIP-READING Principles and Practice". The development and perfecting of this meritorious work on lip-reading was an undertaking...   *How-to Pages 400*

A Handbook of Suggestive Therapeutics, Applied Hypnotism, Psychic Science   ISBN: *1-59462-214-0*   **$24.95**
by Henry Munro   *Health/New Age/Health/Self-help Pages 376*

A Doll's House: and Two Other Plays *by Henrik Ibsen*   ISBN: *1-59462-112-8*   **$19.95**
Henrik Ibsen created this classic when in revolutionary 1848 Rome. Introducing some striking concepts in playwriting for the realist genre, this play has been studied the world over.   *Fiction/Classics/Plays 308*

The Light of Asia *by sir Edwin Arnold*   ISBN: *1-59462-204-3*   **$13.95**
In this poetic masterpiece, Edwin Arnold describes the life and teachings of Buddha. The man who was to become known as Buddha to the world was born as Prince Gautama of India but he rejected the worldly riches and abandoned the reigns of power when... Religion/History/Biographies Pages 170

The Complete Works of Guy de Maupassant *by Guy de Maupassant*   ISBN: *1-59462-157-8*   **$16.95**
"For days and days, nights and nights, I had dreamed of that first kiss which was to consecrate our engagement, and I knew not on what spot I should put my lips..."   *Fiction/Classics Pages 240*

The Art of Cross-Examination *by Francis L. Wellman*   ISBN: *1-59462-309-0*   **$26.95**
Written by a renowned trial lawyer, Wellman imparts his experience and uses case studies to explain how to use psychology to extract desired information through questioning.   *How-to/Science/Reference Pages 408*

Answered or Unanswered? *by Louisa Vaughan*   ISBN: *1-59462-248-5*   **$10.95**
Miracles of Faith in China   *Religion Pages 112*

The Edinburgh Lectures on Mental Science (1909) *by Thomas*   ISBN: *1-59462-008-3*   **$11.95**
This book contains the substance of a course of lectures recently given by the writer in the Queen Street Hail, Edinburgh. Its purpose is to indicate the Natural Principles governing the relation between Mental Action and Material Conditions...   *New Age/Psychology Pages 148*

Ayesha *by H. Rider Haggard*   ISBN: *1-59462-301-5*   **$24.95**
Verily and indeed it is the unexpected that happens! Probably if there was one person upon the earth from whom the Editor of this, and of a certain previ-ous history, did not expect to hear again...   *Classics Pages 380*

Ayala's Angel *by Anthony Trollope*   ISBN: *1-59462-352-X*   **$29.95**
The two girls were both pretty, but Lucy who was twenty-one who supposed to be simple and comparatively unattractive, whereas Ayala was credited, as her Bombwhat romantic name might show, with poetic charm and a taste for romance. Ayala when her father died was nineteen...   Fiction Pages 484

The American Commonwealth *by James Bryce*   ISBN: *1-59462-286-8*   **$34.45**
An interpretation of American democratic political theory. It examines political mechanics and society from the perspective of Scotsman James Bryce   *Politics Pages 572*

Stories of the Pilgrims *by Margaret P. Pumphrey*   ISBN: *1-59462-116-0*   **$17.95**
This book explores pilgrims religious oppression in England as well as their escape to Holland and eventual crossing to America on the Mayflower, and their early days in New England...   *History Pages 268*

QTY

The Fasting Cure *by Sinclair Upton* **ISBN: 1-59462-222-1** **$13.95**
In the Cosmopolitan Magazine for May, 1910, and in the Contemporary Review (London) for April, 1910, I published an article dealing with my experiences in fasting. I have written a great many magazine articles, but never one which attracted so much attention... New Age/Self Help/Health Pages 164

Hebrew Astrology *by Sepharial* **ISBN: 1-59462-308-2** **$13.45**
In these days of advanced thinking it is a matter of common observation that we have left many of the old landmarks behind and that we are now pressing forward to greater heights and to a wider horizon than that which represented the mind-content of our progenitors... Astrology Pages 144

Thought Vibration or The Law of Attraction in the Thought World **ISBN: 1-59462-127-6** **$12.95**
by William Walker Atkinson Psychology/Religion Pages 144

Optimism *by Helen Keller* **ISBN: 1-59462-108-X** **$15.95**
Helen Keller was blind, deaf, and mute since 19 months old, yet famously learned how to overcome these handicaps, and spread her lectures promoting optimism. An inspiring read for everyone... Biographies/Inspirational Pages 84

Sara Crewe *by Frances Burnett* **ISBN: 1-59462-360-0** **$9.45**
In the first place, Miss Minchin lived in London. Her home was a large, dull, tall one, in a large, dull square, where all the houses were alike, and all the sparrows were alike, and where all the door-knockers made the same heavy sound... Childrens/Classic Pages 88

The Autobiography of Benjamin Franklin *by Benjamin Franklin* **ISBN: 1-59462-135-7** **$24.95**
The Autobiography of Benjamin Franklin has probably been more extensively read than any other American historical work, and no other book of its kind has had such ups and downs of fortune. Franklin lived for many years in England, where he was agent... Biographies/History Pages 332

Name	
Email	
Telephone	
Address	
City, State ZIP	

☐ **Credit Card**   ☐ **Check / Money Order**

Credit Card Number	
Expiration Date	
Signature	

Please Mail to: Book Jungle
 PO Box 2226
 Champaign, IL 61825
or Fax to: 630-214-0564

ORDERING INFORMATION

web*: www.bookjungle.com*
email*: sales@bookjungle.com*
fax*: 630-214-0564*
mail*: Book Jungle PO Box 2226 Champaign, IL 61825*
or PayPal *to sales@bookjungle.com*

Please contact us for bulk discounts

DIRECT-ORDER TERMS

**20% Discount if You Order
Two or More Books**
Free Domestic Shipping!
Accepted: Master Card, Visa,
Discover, American Express